This Ladybird Book belongs to:

_____

_____

_____

_____

This Ladybird retelling
by
Molly Perham

Ladybird books are widely available, but in case of
difficulty may be ordered by post or telephone from:

Ladybird Books – Cash Sales Department
Littlegate Road Paignton Devon TQ3 3BE
Telephone 0803 554761

A catalogue record for this book is available
from the British Library

First edition

Published by Ladybird Books Ltd Loughborough Leicestershire UK
Ladybird Books Inc Auburn Maine 04210 USA

Printed in England

FAVOURITE TALES

Peter and
the Wolf

*illustrated
by*
PETER STEVENSON

based on a traditional folk tale

Once upon a time there was a boy
called Peter, who lived with his
grandfather in a house beside a green
meadow. In the forest nearby were all
kinds of dangers.

"You must never go out into the
meadow alone, Peter," warned his
grandfather one day. "The hungry
wolf might come out of the forest and
eat you up."

Peter was not afraid. One sunny morning, he opened the garden gate and went out into the meadow.

A little bird sat high up in a tree.

"Hello, Peter!" chirped the little bird. "What are you doing here all alone?"

"It's such a lovely morning," said Peter, "I'm going for a walk."

Just then a duck came waddling along on her flat, webbed feet. She had followed Peter through the open gate and decided to take a swim in the pond nearby.

Seeing the duck, the little bird flew down to the grass. "Why do you waddle like that?" he asked rudely. "Why don't you fly like me?"

"Who needs to fly?" said the duck. "I can swim!" And she shook out her feathers and dived into the pond. "Come on in," she called. "The water is lovely!"

"You must be joking," twittered the little bird. "I don't swim."

"You mean you *can't* swim," said the duck scornfully.

The little bird hopped up and down with rage.

The duck swam round and round in the water. Peter stood in the long grass and watched as the two birds argued.

Suddenly Peter saw the long grass swaying to and fro. A large striped cat was crawling towards the little bird.

The cat said to himself, "That bird is so busy arguing, he will never see me." And he crept towards the bird on his velvet paws.

"Look out!" warned Peter. Quickly, the bird flew up into a tree.

The duck quacked angrily at the cat from the middle of the pond.

The cat stalked away in a huff. He sat down in the grass and began to wash. "See if I care," he thought. "I'll get that bird next time."

Just then Grandfather came out of the house. When he saw Peter in the meadow, he was very angry.

"What if the wolf should come out of the forest?" Grandfather asked. "What would you do then?"

Peter didn't answer. He was sorry he had disobeyed Grandfather, but he really couldn't see what all the fuss was about.

Grandfather marched Peter back into the garden and locked the gate.

No sooner had Peter gone from the meadow, than the big hungry wolf came out of the forest.

Quick as a flash, the bird flew to the very top of a tree. The cat scrambled up the tree as well.

The duck was so frightened that she jumped right out of the pond.

The wolf saw the duck and ran after
her. She ran as fast as she could,
but the wolf ran faster, and he soon
caught her.

With one gulp, he gobbled her up!

The cat and the little bird sat on a high branch together. The wolf walked round and round the tree, looking at them with greedy eyes.

As Peter watched from behind the gate, he had a very good idea. He knew how to save the cat and the bird.

First Peter found a long rope. Then he climbed the garden wall. When he was sitting safely on top, he began to make a loop in the rope.

Peter called out to the bird, "Fly down and circle round the wolf's head. But don't let him catch you!"

So the little bird flew round and
round, almost touching the wolf's
head with his wings. The wolf
snapped angrily at the bird, and
before long he felt quite dizzy.

Peter quickly finished making the loop in the rope. He let it down carefully, caught the wolf by the tail, and then pulled with all his strength.

The wolf began to jump about wildly, trying to get away. But clever Peter had tied the other end of the rope to the tree. The more the wolf jumped, the tighter the rope became. The wolf simply could not escape.

All at once some hunters, who had
been following the wolf's trail, came
out of the forest. They raised their
guns, ready to fire.

"Don't shoot!" shouted Peter. "The bird and I have caught the wolf. We will take him to the zoo."

The hunters looked up at Peter sitting on the wall, and at the wolf caught fast at the end of the rope. How surprised they were!

That afternoon, Peter led a triumphant procession to the zoo. After Peter came the hunters, leading the wolf. Grandfather followed with the cat, and the little bird flew ahead.

As for the duck, she quacked and quacked inside the wolf. "Don't worry," Peter told her. "I'm sure the zookeepers will set you free."

And they did!

PEUK 3461

Published by Ladybird Books Ltd
A Penguin Company
Penguin Books Ltd, 80 Strand, London, WC2R ORL, England
Penguin Books Australia Ltd, Camberwell, Victoria, Australia
Penguin Group (NZ), cnr Airborne and Rosedale Roads,
Albany, Auckland 1310, New Zealand
All rights reserved

ISBN-13: 978-1-84646-026-5
ISBN-10: 1-8464-6026-3

4 6 8 10 9 7 5

Ladybird and the device of a ladybird are trademarks
of Ladybird Books Ltd

Printed in Italy